This book belongs to

_____

The Emperor's New Clothes

BY

Hans Christian Andersen

Retold by Samantha Easton

ILLUSTRATED BY

Richard Walz

ARIEL BOOKS

ANDREWS AND McMEEL

KANSAS CITY

Library of Congress Cataloging-in-Publication Data

Easton, Samantha.
     The emperor's new clothes / Hans Christian Andersen ; retold by
  Samantha Easton ; illustrated by Richard Walz.
         p.   cm.
     "Ariel books."
     Summary: Two rascals sell a vain emperor an invisible suit of clothes.
     ISBN 0-8362-4928-3 : $6.95
     [1. Fairy tales.] I. Walz, Richard, ill. II. Andersen, H.C. (Hans
  Christian), 1805-1875. Kejserens nye klæder. III. Title.
  PZ8.E135Em   1991
  [E]—dc20   91-13497
                                                                      CIP
First Printing, September 1991   AC
Second Printing, January 1992

Design: Susan Hood and Mike Hortens
Art Direction: Armand Eisen, Mike Hortens, and Julie Phillips
Art Production: Lynn Wine
Production: Julie Miller and Lisa Shadid

The Emperor's
New Clothes

There was once an emperor who loved new clothes. He spent all his money on clothes and had a different suit for every hour of the day. Unlike other emperors, he cared nothing for his soldiers or his fortresses. Nor did he enjoy going to the theater or reading books. No, the emperor loved clothes more than anything else and was always busy adding to his wardrobe.

The emperor lived in a bustling city with a huge marketplace. Visitors came there from all over the world, so it is not surprising that one day two swindlers also arrived.

When these swindlers learned how fond the emperor was of new clothes, they let it be known that they were famous weavers and that the cloth they made was the finest in the world. Not only were the colors and patterns remarkably beautiful, but the cloth possessed a magical quality. Clothes made from it were completely invisible to anyone who was a fool or unfit for his or her job.

Soon everyone in the city was talking about the marvelous cloth, and of course the emperor came to hear about it, too.

"A suit made of such cloth would be a wonderful thing to have!" the emperor thought. "With a suit like that I would be able to tell at once who was clever and who was stupid and whether the people in my court were really fit for their jobs. I must order a suit of this cloth at once!"

10

So the emperor summoned the two swindlers to his palace. Then he gave them a large bag of gold so that they would begin work right away.

The swindlers set up their looms in a room in the palace. They ordered the finest silk in all the colors of the rainbow and thread of silver and gold. But they did not use any of this. Instead, they hid it all away. Then they pretended to be hard at work on their empty looms.

After a time the emperor wondered how the marvelous cloth was coming along. He was about to go see for himself, when he remembered that the cloth would be invisible to anyone who was a fool or unfit for his or her office.

Now, the emperor was quite sure he himself had nothing to worry about. Nevertheless, he thought it might be wise to send someone else to look at the cloth first. "I shall send my honest old minister to look at it," the emperor thought. "He's very clever, and he knows his job better than anyone!"

So the honest old minister went to the room where the swindlers were working.

The minister entered the room and was startled to see the swindlers bent over empty looms. "Goodness gracious!" he thought. "I can't see anything at all!" He rubbed his eyes and opened them as wide as possible.

But it did no good. He could not see even a thread of the marvelous cloth.

"Oh, no!" the honest old minister thought. "I never would have believed it. Can it be that I'm a fool or unfit for my position?"

The thought of it was so dreadful that the old minister decided not to say a word about his experience to anyone.

"Do tell us what you think of our lovely cloth," said the swindlers as they bent over their looms.

"It . . . it is very beautiful, indeed," stammered the minister. "What fine colors! What an exquisite pattern! I've never seen anything like it!"

"We thought you would be impressed," said the swindlers. They described the colors and unusual pattern in great detail. The minister listened very carefully so that he would be able to repeat every word to the emperor. Then he went and told the emperor that the cloth was truly marvelous—the finest he had ever seen.

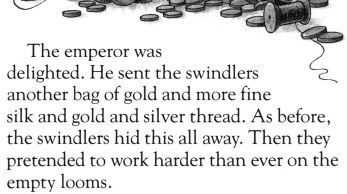

The emperor was delighted. He sent the swindlers another bag of gold and more fine silk and gold and silver thread. As before, the swindlers hid this all away. Then they pretended to work harder than ever on the empty looms.

A while later, the emperor again wondered how the marvelous cloth was coming.

This time the emperor decided to send his most trusted courtier to have a look at it.

Like the old minister before him, the courtier looked and looked and rubbed his eyes and looked again. But no matter what he did, he could see nothing at all.

"Don't you find the cloth exquisite?" asked the swindlers. "Have you ever seen such colors or such a pattern before?"

"How can this be?" the courtier thought. "I know I am not stupid. Can I be unfit for my position? How terrible! I must not let anyone know of this!"

So the courtier praised the cloth highly. "Never have I seen anything to compare with it!" he said. And that was exactly what he told the emperor.

Now, everyone in the city could speak of nothing but the marvelous cloth. So the emperor decided to go see it for himself.

The emperor, followed by all his courtiers and ministers, went to the swindlers' room. When the emperor walked in, the swindlers appeared to be hard at work over the empty looms.

"Isn't the cloth breathtaking!" said the honest old minister. "Has your majesty ever seen such a delicate and unusual pattern?" On and on he went, imagining that all the others could see the beautiful cloth.

The emperor blinked and rubbed his eyes. But he could see nothing at all! "Oh, dear," he thought. "Can I be a fool? Am I unfit to be emperor? This is the worst thing that has ever happened to me! No one must ever suspect!"

Then he said to the swindlers, "I couldn't

be more delighted. The cloth is absolutely
. . . magnificent!"

"Stupendously beautiful!" chimed his
courtiers. "Excellent in every way," said his
ministers. Then they advised the emperor to
order a suit of the cloth to be ready to wear
in the great procession planned for that very
week.

So the emperor did. He gave the swindlers
even more gold and appointed them Royal
Weavers to the Empire.

On the day before the procession, the two
swindlers appeared to be working frantically
to finish the emperor's new suit.

All day long they cut through the air with
scissors and sewed with needles that had no

thread. Everyone noticed that the candles in their workroom burned all night long. At last, when morning came, the swindlers announced, "The emperor's suit is now finished!"

The emperor, followed by the entire court, proceeded to the swindlers' room.

The swindlers bowed when the emperor entered. Then they held up their empty hands. "Look," they said. "Here is the

emperor's new jacket." And "Here is the emperor's new vest." And "Here are the emperor's new trousers."

All the courtiers and ministers nodded their heads in wonder. "What a beautiful suit," they all said. "Truly splendid!"

The emperor nodded, too. "Yes, indeed," he said. "I couldn't be more pleased."

"And see how cleverly the suit is made," the swindlers said. "Feel this jacket. It is as

23

light as air!"

"Why, yes, so it is," said the emperor.

"Now," said the swindlers, "will your majesty be so kind as to undress please, so that your majesty may put on your new suit of clothes?"

They led the emperor to a large mirror. Then they helped him take off his clothes and pretended to put on his new suit piece by piece—first the trousers, then the shirt, then the vest, and then the jacket.

"There!" they exclaimed when they were done. "Doesn't the new suit fit your majesty to perfection?"

The emperor stared at himself in the mirror. He could not see a thing, but he dared not admit it.

"Ah, yes," he said, admiring his reflection. "It looks very nice. Doesn't my new suit become me?" he asked his courtiers and ministers.

"Oh, yes," they agreed. "Your majesty
has never looked so splendid in any other
clothes."

"And does the pattern really suit me?"
asked the emperor, feeling a little uneasy.

"No other pattern could possibly suit you
so well!" said his courtiers.

"Very true," said his ministers.

Then the servants who were to carry the
emperor's train stepped forward.

As they could not see the cloth,
they pretended to hold the train

in their hands, and the procession began.

The emperor marched under his splendid red velvet canopy, and his servants and footman marched after him. He marched out of the palace gates and through the city streets.

The streets were lined with people, for everyone wanted to see the emperor's new clothes.

As the emperor passed, everyone cried, "Look how splendid the emperor's new suit is! Such colors! Such a pattern!"

Not a one of them dared let their neighbors know that he could see nothing. They might be thought fools or unfit for their jobs, and that would be dreadful!

So they all praised the emperor's new clothes as loudly as they could. Never had any of the emperor's clothes caused such a stir. Then a small child cried out, "But, Mother, the emperor has nothing on!"

"Shhh," said the child's mother. But then she looked again at the emperor, and said, "Why, it's true. The emperor has nothing on!"

One of her neighbors overheard her, and began shouting it, too. Then all the people shouted at once, "But the emperor has nothing on!"

The emperor could not help hearing them. He blushed bright red, for he realized it was true. But what could he do? So he stood up even straighter and kept walking, wearing only his crown and underclothes. Meanwhile the emperor's servants marched behind him, holding his imaginary train as if nothing were wrong. And so ends the story of the emperor's new clothes!